WRITER

BY LILLY BUCHANAN

Writer
1975
Lilly Buchanan

Writer

Lilly Buchanan

Published by Lilly Buchanan, 2024.

This is a work of fiction. Similarities to real people, places, or events are entirely coincidental.

WRITER

First edition. August 22, 2024.

Copyright © 2024 Lilly Buchanan.

ISBN: 979-8227510860

Written by Lilly Buchanan.

To my Brother Jason White. You inspire me to follow my dreams. I love you!

Dedicated to my Brother Jason White. You inspire me to follow my dreams! I love you!

Avery Lawson's first book sold over 2 million copies. She went on to make over 22 million dollars in book sales in her career. She praises a wonderful financial adviser, Miquel Vasques, who made very lucrative investments for her. Over time, Avery's network climbed into close to a 75-million-dollar range. Avery never complained about making money or having money, however, marketing the books annually nearly did her in. She truly had no idea how difficult it would be on her mind and body, touring around America and other countries.

She despised being on television or radio talk shows. The interviewers were given a list of topics she would discuss and were asked not to deviate from those topics, yet there was always someone trying to make a name for themselves, trying to get an exclusive. She had learned over time to openly say, "We agreed not to bring that topic up, or I did not agree to approach that topic when I agreed to this interview." If the interviewer continued to push her, Avery would remove her microphone and say, "Excuse me please," and leave the set, abruptly leaving the interview. The spiteful media had labeled her uncooperative and hard to work with. It didn't matter they were attempting to dive into her privacy. For instance, when she and Ian broke up, she was heartbroken. He left her for the next-door neighbor's 21-year-old daughter. Someone leaked it to the press (probably Ian) and Avery refused to discuss it. In her eyes, Ian didn't leave her for the child, he left her for another woman. It was painful and humiliating.

The fact that all the trash magazines thought it newsworthy, made her sick. To her credit, she held herself to a standard and stood on that standard. Avery's nerves were always frazzled by the time the quick interviews were over. If those interviews made it to the end, they were exhaustive. Noone valued her privacy. She had to fight her agent about sitting for interviews. She hated them.

She couldn't sleep in those expensive hotels, and she knew she could not go for a walk, as the crime was terrible in large cities. She also knew that reporters were always camped out to find her doing something immoral, illegal, or irresponsible. Her agent constantly warned her to use caution. She felt trapped all of the time. When she arrived back in New York after 16 major cities book tour; she told her publisher... "I'm exhausted. I did your book tour. Now I am taking a long, well-earned sabbatical."

The publisher looked upset and said, "Avery, I've got some bad news. Your biological parents have been in touch. They want to meet with you."

"Absolutely not!" Avery screamed. "They gave me away to an orphanage when I was 7 years old. Now that my books have sold millions of copies, they want access to my money. If they had wanted a relationship before, I might have considered their olive branch, but not now."

"They said if you meet with them, they won't go to the press about your past." "Roger, I was 7 years old. What kind of past could I possibly have?"

"They stated that you were promiscuous." "Roger, I don't care if they tell that to everyone in the world. It is an outrageous lie. Meant to slander me and blackmail me. They just want money."

"Okay, I will put our attorneys on it. Maybe it would be good for you to disappear for a while. Go get some rest and write a new book."

Avery stared blankly at him, smiled, and walked out of his office. She was so tired her eyeballs hurt. Sometimes she forgot that she was only a money maker to Roger. "Write a new book." He called after her.

She shook her head. "What a creep." She thought to herself.

Before Avery arrived downstairs to her private car, her cell phone rang, it was Roger. "I forgot to tell you Hollywood wants to do a movie about your latest book." "No Roger. For no amount of money and if they make one even similar to it...sue them." "Yes ma'am. I told everyone you wouldn't agree to it. I am obligated to tell you, that they are offering mega amounts of money and offering you total creative control. You even get to pick the actors." Avery hung up the telephone. As she entered the car, she felt something break inside of her. She thought she was having a heart attack.

Her chest was tight and even her neck and left arm felt numb. She was sweating and breathing hard, then she began to cry and gasp for air. The driver calmly asked if she needed a doctor.

She shook her head yes and said, "But please don't take me to a hospital." My brother is a doctor ma'am and I can have him come here to see you in this car." Avery nodded yes, but could not speak due to the crying. "Take me away from here please."

He drove a couple of miles away, all while calling his brother to meet them. Miraculously, his brother was nearby. In a few minutes, the back door opened and the driver's brother stepped in. He spoke softly to Avery. He took her blood pressure and listened to her heartbeat. He saw she was still sweating.

He wiped her brow and gave her an aspirin and water. He checked her pulse. "Your heart rate is high, but I am sure you had a panic attack. They resemble heart attacks, but it is panic. Have you received bad news today?" "Yes," she whispered. "I'm going to suggest you take a break from whatever is upsetting you.

Here is a prescription for anxiety medication. It will help when the panic attacks come or I can hospitalize you..."

"No, please. I can't be hospitalized. The publicity would crush me." She said through her sobs. "I'm going away for a vacation. That will help."

"Do you feel like harming yourself or anyone else?" he asked quietly.

"No sir. I think I am just tired. I just completed a 16-city tour for my book. I'm exhausted. Thank you so much for coming. Please send the bill to Sanderson Publishing."

"Okay but promise me if those thoughts enter your mind, you will seek help."

"I promise."

"Where are you going to get rest?" he asked.

"I have a home in the Bahamas. No one knows me there. I can be off-radar."

"Do you have any friends there?" the doctor asked.

"No sir. I am sort of a loner. I'm a writer. My computers and my notebooks are my friends." Avery said with a sad sigh. "Okay, well, let's get this prescription filled first and you can take it with you. I'm prescribing plenty of rest and not a lot of alcohol. Eat clean, and relax. Things are never as bad as they seem.

Read some books, watch some movies, walk on the beach. Here is my private number if you need someone to talk to." He said with a concerned look was on his face.

"I will follow the doctors' orders," Avery said with half of a smile. The pain in her chest was easing up, and her breath was beginning to feel normal again. She had the driver take her to the closest pharmacy. The driver went in and got the prescription filled for her, then they went to the airport. Avery used her fake passport and identification that was named after one of her characters. Her publisher had gotten them for her, to hide her from the press. She boarded Sanderson Publishing's private jet and flew to Miami. From Miami, she took a smaller plane to her home on North Andros, Bahamas. Her house was a stunning waterfront property. That waterfront was the Atlantic Ocean. She paid to have that house-built years ago. Roger staffed it with a cook, a masseur, a housekeeper, an assistant, a car and driver, 2 gardeners, and a Property Manager to look after the horses and livestock. She was thankful when the flying was over. It always made her very anxious. It was so great to see her house again. She loved her library. She had shipped hand-picked books to go into the library and it had a way of making her smile every time she walked in. 50% of the books were autographed, and the other half was written by deceased authors. Philipa Gregory was one of Avery's favorite authors. Avery had all of Mrs. Gregory's books. She was her literary hero. Once at the house, Avery didn't sleep well, and when she did, she had bad dreams, regarding Roger's news about her birth parents.

She was reliving the nightmare of her youth and she knew the birth parents would sell their story to the highest bidder. America loves to hear dirt on anyone, so they can write about it or broadcast it on television. She started to feel like she was having another panic attack, and then she remembered the pills the doctor prescribed. She took one and lay across her bed. It did seem to calm her down. She cried softly. 'Why couldn't those people leave her alone? All she had done was make something good out of her life. Why did they have to try to ruin it for her?' Her cell phone rang. She looked at the number, it was her driver." "Richard? Is everything okay?" "Yes, ma'am. My brother, Samuel, the doctor, is here and he is concerned for you. Would you mind speaking to him?" "No, I don't mind." Samuel came on the line. "Miss Avery. Richard would not give me your number. I just wanted to check on you. Is the medication working okay for you? Have you had any more panic attacks?" "Yes, as a matter of fact, I had another one about 30 minutes ago and I remembered the pills and took one. I'm not great at taking care of myself Samuel. I always have somewhere to be or something to do." Samuel said, "Listen, I know you don't know me too well, but I have a few days

off. Would it be okay if I fly over and just visit with you? It seems like you need a friend right now. I have no plans. You would save me from countless hours of studying medical journals and taking naps." Avery laughed. "I uh, I can't promise you an exciting time, and you did prescribe rest." "Yes, I did. However, I did not prescribe complete solitude."

"Okay, that sounds nice. I will see you when you get here. Thanks for this. It is very kind of you."

"I will see you soon Avery." And he hung up. Avery was a little excited, but she also assumed he was just being a good doctor.

He had come to make sure she was not having a heart attack in the car, maybe he was just following up on her health. She didn't know when the last time a man was truly interested in her. She always pushed them away when they got too close. It was like she had this superpower of listening too close. Men would slip up and say stupid things, but telling truths. Their intentions were not honorable. "Baby when we get married, we are gonna have 12 kids and you can stay home and cook me dinner every night." "Wait! What?" "When we get married, we are gonna live in Las Vegas and party every night.

It's just gonna be a blast from then on out. We can live on room service and casino buffets." Or her personal favorite, "I won't ever have to work again and you can keep on cranking out those books of yours." Every man she had ever met just wanted her money, not her. She finally gave up. She finally quit letting it break her heart and withdrew into herself and her craft. She had not dated in over 3 years. Occasionally she did wish she had someone she could lean on, like right now. This thing with her biological parents surfacing was a thorn in her side. She wished she had changed her total identity when she first became famous.

Mrs. Palance, from the orphanage, had adopted her when she was 10 years old, so legally she was Avery's legal parent. However, when she died, and the truth was buried with her. The name Avery Palance died when her publisher and agent, Roger, had asked her to use the name Avery Lawson as her pen name. She agreed because she wanted him to publish her book. It turned out to be a fantastic thing to do. She could think of over 85 million reasons why it had turned out to be a great idea. Avery started to shake, her hands were trembling and she could not stop them. How could these horrible people resurface? She had barely survived them as a child. "Please, not again." She pleaded with God. "Please spare me the chaos and insanity that those 2 people bring."

When Avery was 7 years old, she loved to read. The library was her safe place. She could dive inside each book and escape her miserable life. Noone humiliated her, hit her, or called her filthy names like her drunken parents did. Everyone who worked at the library was kind and made Avery feel welcome.

One evening while visiting the library, Mrs. Teddom, the librarian asked Avery if she could stay and push in the chairs and put a few books back on the shelf. Avery was eager to do the tasks and thanked Mrs. Teddom for letting her help.

When she completed her errand, they said goodnight, and Mrs.. Teddom locked the door as she left. Avery began her walk home. A car full of older boys drove slowly past her. They called out to her and offered her a ride, to which she said, "No thank you." She kept her head down and continued to walk faster. She was within 2 blocks of her home when the car came back and the boys grabbed her and forced her into their car.

When Avery regained consciousness, she was on her front lawn. Her panties were in a knot around one of her ankles, and her dress was gone. She had one sock on, and the other was missing. Avery was in severe pain. She was so dizzy and in agonizing pain. She couldn't get up from the ground. She had been beaten severely. Her legs were so damaged that the doctors said she would forever walk with a limp. A neighbor found her. She beat fiercely on Avery's parent's door to let them know their child was injured. Avery's drunken parents began screaming at her and humiliating her. "Don't be bothering us about that girl. She's trouble." Her father screamed at the neighbor. "But she is hurt." The neighbor screamed back. Her father came out and looked at her laying there. Her father spit on her and went back into his house, and slammed the door. He left Avery on the lawn, but not before calling her a whore and other filthy names. The neighbor ran and got a sheet to cover her up. She screamed for her husband to call the police, and an ambulance. The police arrived before the ambulance. The officer nearly broke down when he saw Avery in that condition. He tried to console her, explaining, "We are going to get you to the hospital. Don't be scared honey. The doctors will be able to help you." The police officer wanted to break down so bad. He really wanted to kick in Avery's parents door and choke both of them for their behavior during this atrocity. He was very familiar with them. Their neighbors had telephoned many times about the drunken brawls.

This was different. Crimes against children were his weakness. He hated them.

Avery stayed in the hospital for 4 weeks. Avery's hips and both of her legs were broken and one of her legs had to be rebroken to be set correctly into a cast. Her parents never came to see her one time in the hospital.

Even though Avery eventually described the car to the police, no one was ever charged with the crimes that happened to her. She could not remember what the boys looked like. The police brought books of mug shots to show her, but she didn't recognize any of the pictures. Not one stood out to her.

Once Mrs.. Palance met Avery's parents, she felt more pangs of sympathy for this child. Both parents were stinking drunk at 10 am the morning she visited. The father berated the mother and Avery. "She is her mother's daughter all right. Her mother has been with most of the men in this town, just for a lousy drink." The mother was quiet and did not defend herself against his slander.

Mrs. Palance said, "Look, I am not here to argue who is this or that. If you will just sign these papers, you will no longer have to be concerned with the child." Both parents signed immediately without reading the papers. "Is there any kind of money we get for signing these papers?" the mother asked. Mrs. Palance was shocked. No one had ever asked for money in exchange for their child. Mrs. Palance opened her purse and took out $40.00 (forty dollars). They both looked like hungry tigers going after the money. The father snatched the money before the mother could get it. "I'll take that. Good riddance I say." The father said with a laugh, "She is your dirty little problem now. And you tell her not to darken our door again, EVER. She has disgraced us."

Mrs. Palance nearly bit her tongue off to keep from saying what she thought. She picked up the paper bag with a few pairs of threadbare underwear, one dirty dress, a broken doll, and 3 books. Mrs. Palance wanted to cry when she saw what was in the bag as she placed it in the taxi.

'My orphanage will be a million times better for any child, than for one to live in that den of drunks.' She thought to herself.

Miss Gertrude Palance came to pick up Avery from the hospital. "Avery, I am Miss Gertrude Palance. I run a girls' orphanage about 40 miles north of here. Your parents have signed over their parental rights, meaning they don't want to be your parents anymore. Your father believes you to be promiscuous and that you did this to yourself by flirting with boys." Avery was still under the influence of pain medication, however, she managed to whisper, "Ma'am, I didn't do nothin' wrong. I remember I was at the library and Miss Teddom asked me to help her tidy up in the library as it closed. She locked the door when I left. I was walking home and a blue car offered me a ride. I said no thank you. I can remember the car driving back around and somebody jumped out, somebody grabbed my hair and drug me into the car. I was kicking and fighting. He put a rag over my face. It smelled sweet. I guess I went to sleep when he did that because when I woke up, I was here. You can ask Miss Teddom about me helping at the library."

"She has already confirmed everything dear. It's over now. You will do fine at the girl's home. There are other girls with whom you can become best friends. They will be like your sisters. Avery you will be happy there. I love every child that I have in my care." Avery sighed and said, "Yes ma'am." as she drifted off to sleep. Mrs. Palance was not normally so sympathetic to a girl's past, however this attack on a child so young tore at her heart strings, not to mention the derelict's who were her birth parents.

Eventually the hospital released Avery into Mrs. Palance's care. Mrs. Palance and her staff would provide a very good and happy home for Avery. They provided music lessons, art lessons, and lessons on manners. The girls were taught history, math, and English literature. Some girls were interested in science. They were allowed tutors for that specific subject. Avery wanted to be a writer. Mrs. Palance encouraged each child to follow their dreams. If any child did any kind of chore, they were paid 10 cents per chore at the end of the week. Avery loved to volunteer to help, and she made many friends at the orphanage. The food was delicious, the staff was nice to each of them and Mrs. Palance was a wonderful, kind person. Each child was special and loved. On Sunday they had church and a big dinner. It was not forced, it was love. Avery learned that love was not meant to be hard and unbearable.

Avery couldn't stop shaking. She suddenly missed Mrs. Palance so much. She had died tragically of a stroke when Avery was 15. The relatives of Mrs. Palance who took over the orphanage were awful. They fired all the staff and used Avery and all the other children as slave labor, forcing them to cook, take in laundry from the public, and clean other people's houses. The meals were meager, leaving each child hungry constantly.

Avery was living off of 4 hours of sleep a night. The new owners were cruel to the children. It was a different orphanage once they took over. Avery stayed for 2 more years, then she packed a suitcase and snuck out into the night. She went to the police station and reported how the new owners were abusing the children and not feeding them properly.

The Police Captain listened to her and promised to investigate her complaint. Four days later, Avery saw a newspaper headline; the orphanage had been shut down and all of the children were placed in foster homes. The new owners were charged with cruelty and abuse.

Avery caught a bus to New York. She was hoping to put her past behind her.

A new life might stop the nightmares, shaking and hopelessness she sometimes experienced. New York was a long way from Pension, Arizona, but Avery didn't care. She was starting a new life. Miraculously Avery found work in a public library. It didn't pay a lot; however, they also allowed her to work in their corner bookstore on the weekends to make extra money. Avery did not mind working 7 days a week because she loved working around books. It was her passion. She dreamed of her own book being on the shelves one day. Another bonus was if she wanted to check out a book she could, that was medicine to her heart.

The library gave her used paper, that was clean on the opposite side for her to write her short stories on, since she could not afford to purchase her own paper yet. They were very supportive of her and her desire to write. The assistant librarian would critique and edit Avery's stories. Avery felt like a real writer, when she received the stories back and they were marked with corrections. It inspired her.

Avery had a tiny apartment and she loved it. It was her first home. A safe place where she could relax and be happy. Each payday she went to a local thrift store and bought a few things at a time for her home, curtains, cooking utensils, a frying pan, a pot to boil things in, and a few books. It was like heaven. No one was being mean to her, it was her home, her rules.

FREEDOM

Avery loved her vacation home in the Bahamas; she felt a sense of relief. Her publisher and accountant convinced her to build it three years ago, as a tax write-off. However, it more than a tax write off, it was a safe haven. There was no pressure there. No paparazzi, no trespassers. Just sun, sand, rest, and freedom to do anything she wanted and not be disturbed. The house had a gorgeous ocean view, she was in love with it. Avery felt a peace inside of that home.

There were huge deep blue holes in the ocean close to her beaches that people could dive into, but not Avery...she did not know how to swim and she didn't want to learn. What is the irony, a woman who owns a piece of an amazing island, can't swim? It was her prerogative.

No one seemed to know she was a very rich, famous author. If they did, they never let it be known. The housekeeper and cook, Mrs. Ohara, gave strict orders to the rest of the staff that Avery was not to be bothered.

Avery was moved that Samuel was coming to join her. It was a little lonely taking in all that beauty with no one to share it with. Frankly, no one had cared how she felt for a very long time. It was refreshing to know someone cared.

Mrs. Ohara brought her a beautiful fruit salad with grilled chicken, the dressing was on the side and a pina colada to relax her.

She wasn't very hungry but she did her best to try and eat to not hurt Mrs. Ohara's feelings. After lunch, Avery tried to take a nap on the chaise lounge on her huge porch. The warmth of the sun felt so good on her skin. She was drowsy when Mrs. Ohara came to get the tray.

"Little Miss, if you haven't put on sunscreen, that sun gone burn you up. Your skin is white as milk."

Avery giggled and said, "You are right Mrs. Ohara. I will go inside and see if I can take a nap."

Avery slept fitfully for not very long, in her bed. She called for a massage and they sent the lady masseur over. In the middle of the massage, Avery fell asleep and she dreamed she was kissing Samuel. When she awoke, she took a shower and put on a pretty, long sundress and sandals. Samuel arrived at 8 PM just in time for dinner. Thinking about her dream, she remembered Samuel was tall, and muscular, black hair and grey eyes. He was really handsome, and a doctor. That is a nice package. He arrived and hugged her neck. "I got here as quick as I could. Did I miss anything?" Avery giggled and said "No. But, I am so glad you came here, Samuel. I have been feeling a little lost, maybe even lonely. Thank you for coming."

"It is truly my pleasure, Avery." He said with a smile. "How are you feeling?" "Still a little tired. I'm still not sleeping well." "Maybe you just need to talk. Sometimes that helps." Avery blushed and said, "Not right now, for goodness sakes, you just got here. Why don't we have dinner?

Mrs. Ohara cooked a great meal." Samuel said, "That is wonderful. I'm starving."

Mrs. Ohara served the dinner. When he was not looking, Mrs. Ohara cut her eyes at him. Something was off about his character. She had a gift for seeing these things. She hoped Little Miss would be cautious with him. Dinner was amazing, shrimp, scallops, and lobster, scalloped potatoes and a slaw salad. Samuel and Avery went for a walk on the beach after dinner. The moon was beautiful and lighting up the beach. It would have been a very romantic scene for two lovers. But they were not lovers. They were just beginning to be friends.

Avery collected a few sea shells as they walked along the beach. "This is great. I have never collected the shells before. I never paid them much attention before I guess."

"Yes, sometimes we are so busy, that we overlook the beauty right in front of us," Samuel answered sadly. "Have you done any self-care while being here Avery?" he asked.

"Yes, sir. I had a very therapeutic massage and I had a beautiful fruit salad for lunch with grilled chicken, then I tried to take a nap on the chaise lounge on the beach but was chased back inside by the housekeeper who said I would burn up if I stayed out too long because I am white as a ghost or something to that nature. I came inside and tried to luxurious nap but ended up sleeping restlessly for about 45 minutes. I took a long bubble bath after you called, that relaxed me. I haven't had any caffeine at all. So yes, I've been good to myself so far."

Samuel took her hand and said, "I am so proud of you. Sometimes it takes practice and special effort to be kind to ourselves. You can do it."

Avery said, "Yes especially when you have been pushed and shoved through 16 cities of a book tour. I assume that is why I am still exhausted."

"That is a lot, Avery. You need to set boundaries with your publisher and agent."

"Yes. I can see that now. The 16-city tour was fast, furious and too much. I didn't even know what city I was in most of the time. I ate nothing but hotel food in my room. My nerves are shot from other things we haven't spoken about yet."

"Well after breakfast in the morning, let's plan on talking," Samuel said. "I've got large shoulders and I swear all of your secrets are safe with me."

Avery smiled at him. She wondered to herself, 'What is the magic in him and other doctors that made them care so much for other people and their problems?' She wished she had that magic in her, but then come to think of it, she had sold over 22 million books, she had her own kind of magic and had reached people all over the world. She thought to herself, "'Maybe each of us is given a portion of magic and it is up to us, how we use that magic. Some use it for good, others use it for evil." Avery watched as it softly began to rain.

"When you are feeling stronger and it's not raining, I can take you to see if there is sea glass from the beach. You will enjoy that." Samuel said. "I would love that," Avery said aloud still staring out at the beautiful ocean. They walked back into the house. Mrs. Ohara, the cook, was waiting for her husband to come and pick her up from work. "Hello!" Avery said. The housekeeper and cook, looked startled, "Hello Little Miss." "I have to tell you; my meals today were amazing. Thank you so much. I know your secret ingredient."

The cook blurted out, "You do?" Avery smiled and said, "It's love, isn't it."

Mrs. Ohara laughed and said, "Yes, it is Little Miss. I love to cook and I love to see people to enjoy my cooking." Avery smiled and touched her arm, "You truly have a gift and I am so proud to have you working here." Mrs. Ohara beamed with pride and said, "It is my honor, Little Miss."

A car came slowly around the corner and stopped in front of them. An elderly Mr. Ohara got out and took his hat off and said, "The Queen's chariot has arrived." The ladies giggled, and then Mrs. Ohara climbed into the car next to her husband. It was fun, yet Avery felt a sad as they drove away.

She had never met the right man and she had been single for 5 long years. Her longing for a relationship was always in her writing. Those characters always wound up happily married.

Samuel asked, May I ask why they call you Little Miss?" "It's an island thing I guess, because they all call me that. I think it's sweet." Samuel said, "Well, I happen to feel that its belittling. Not sure I approve of that." Avery looked at him and said, "I am fine with it. I find it endearing." She found it odd that he thought his opinion mattered. Samuel just looked at her strangely, and turn to go shower and get ready for bed.

Avery went back into the house and picked up one of her notebooks to write down a few things that were swirling around in her head. If she didn't write it down, it would disappear and be lost to her. She could never recall ideas, once they left. She had a strange feeling in the pit of her stomach. She wondered why she allowed a stranger into her home?

Once Mrs. Palance and Avery arrived at the Orphanage, Avery was given a downstairs room as she could not climb the stairs. She had to stay in bed for another 7 weeks, however, the girls all came one by one to meet her. This kept their curiosity down and was a chance for Avery to bond with the girls. Eventually she graduated to a wheel chair, which the girls took turns pushing her around. Avery had extensive damage from the attack. Her body was broken but amazingly not her little spirit. The girls brought her dolls, and puzzles, and sat and talked with her for hours, telling her their stories. Avery and all of the girls got along famously and they all felt love and a peace there with Mrs. Palance. She told Avery to say she was in a car accident. Avery agreed. The library sent over books for Avery to read during her recovery. The librarian, Mrs. Teddom, who Avery had stayed to assist that horrible night she was attacked, made it her business to donate money to Mrs. Palance' home every payday to help Avery, until the day she died, which was 5 years later. Many said her guilt killed her.

Mrs. Palance had always appreciated the donations and books for the children. One evening while sitting at her desk, working on Avery's file, the telephone rang. It was Dr. Pein. "Mrs. Palance, I have some information I need to share with you regarding Avery. Would you rather come to my office or shall I tell you over the telephone?" "It's okay Dr. Pein, you can tell me over the telephone." "Okay, please know we have concluded all of our research and the police their investigation. This is rather graphic information. Avery truly was viciously sexually assaulted and attacked. There was extensive damage done to her little insides and chances are good that she will never have children when she grows up. She will walk again, but will always have a limp. She will transition from a wheelchair to a cane but I have no idea how long the process will take, so you will need to be patient with her progress. We will send a physical therapist to work with her during these next 3 weeks of bed rest. Also, I want you to know, that our test has proven that the attackers used Chloroform, probably on a rag, to knock her out. Hopefully, she will never remember all that happened to her. They savagely raped her, then used objects to puncture her little body. This is the worst case I have ever seen in my life and my heart breaks for that child."

Mrs. Palance was crying as she said, "Dr. Pein, thank you so much for calling me and letting me know what happened to Avery. She is a very sweet girl and did not deserve this. I will take good care of her. Please put the details in your report in case she ever needs it when she grows up."

"I will and Mrs. Palance, I am serious, if you ever need medical advice or financial help, please do not hesitate to call me and I will come to you and Avery."

"Thank you, Dr. Pein. I promise you; I will take good care of Avery. Thank you for calling."

Mrs. Palance put a piece of paper in her typewriter and typed out everything the doctor had reported to her. Tears were rolling down her face as she typed the report. She covered the report with a blank sheet of paper then put it in Averys file.

Samuel went back to New York after his brief stay. He assured Avery that he was a phone call away. They had some tense talks about her childhood, and her life as an adult, and he felt that she would be a lot better since she got the burdens off of her chest. Avery wasn't sure if she could really trust Samuel.

She only gave him surface information. Nothing deep. Nothing he could throw in her face if he became angry with her.

He encouraged her to tell her publisher to hire an attorney to sue the offending party (her birth parents) and if they continued to contact her agency, and to call the police and file harassment charges. After Samuel left, she called Roger, the publisher, and told him exactly what Samuel had suggested.

"I hope you have thought this through. The gossip magazines will try to ruin you." Roger replied quietly. "Roger, there are police reports and medical reports to back up my attack. I am not afraid of them anymore. Please tell the attorney to sue them for defamation if they sell their story to anyone."

Rodger said, "I don't know what kind of vitamins you are taking Avery, but you are sounding stronger than I have ever known you to be. Good for you. We will turn the tables on these idiots and they will run for the hills."

"Yes, I want them to keep away from my good name." "I'm calling our attorney Frank Collins right now. By the way, have you written anything? I'd love to proof it." "Goodbye Roger," Avery said with a giggle as she hung up the telephone. She was writing but she didn't want to encourage Roger or he would be harassing her about letting him see her new ideas. He did that with every single book she ever wrote. She was going to keep her new works under wrap until she felt they were ready to be published.

Avery made a point every day to go and visit the horses. They seemed to respond to her with affection and it thrilled Avery to spend time with them.

Mr. Peterson, the property manager and horse's groom, enjoyed seeing Avery with the horses. She was very careful and seemed mesmerized by them. She was very sincere and humble. He would walk the horses to the corral, then hand the reins to Avery and she would walk them around. Avery noticed the horses were not wild, they seemed to have manners. They moved gingerly, as to not stress Avery. She loved to brush them, although she had to stand on a box to brush their backs. She spoke gently to the horses and they seemed enchanted by her. For 5 weeks, Avery had spent quality time with them and they seemed to love her.

Contrary to her last conversation with Roger, Avery was writing more in her notebooks. Mrs. Ohara continued to make wonderful meals. It felt like home. A feeling Avery had not known her entire adult life.

She always felt a new story wanting to come out but she didn't want to overwhelm her mind. She wrote down the idea of the stories. Normally she wrote at night in her notebooks, in her bedroom, not in the office with a typewriter or computer.

But lately during the day, when she was in the office, looking out at the ocean, she was intensively writing with a passion.

She and Mr. Peterson walked on the beach about 3 times a week and she had collected a lot of sea glass. It was beautiful. She kept the glass pieces in a jar on her dresser, that Mr. Peterson had given her for her collection. Samuel had offered but never followed through with his offer. Mr. Peterson was very nice. He seemed a little reserved, but he was friendly. She figured he was about 50-something years old. He was very handsome and had impeccable manners. His British accent made her heart flutter. He had blue eyes and blonde hair that was graying at the temple. He was very handsome; oh, I guess I've already said that once before.

"Mr. Peterson, if you don't mind me asking, how did you come to Andros Island? He smiled, then said, "I am originally from Belfast. My father saw I was running with the wrong crowd and he sent me to live in Manchester with my mother. She had remarried and her new husband made sure I didn't feel welcomed. I stayed for 2 years; until I was 17. Then I lied about my age, telling the government I was 18 and I joined the British Armed Forces. It was good for me. The direction and structure made a man of me. I retired after 25 years of service. I answered an advertisement about managing this farm and we agreed on a salary. I have been here for 10 years."

That is quite an inspirational story, sir! Thank you for your service." Mr. Peterson chuckled and said, "It was my pleasure. It made a responsible man out of me. Anything you would like to share?"

"Well let's see, I love your horses. I love to read. Oh, and Mrs.. Ohara's cooking is going to make me fat." She said with a giggle. He chuckled and said, "Let's go to the barn. I have a surprise for you." "I hope it is a good surprise."

"You will love it." Mr. Peterson said with a smile.

Once they arrived back at the barn, Mr. Peterson whistled and called all of the horses. They were in their stalls so they put their heads out. "Okay, guys. Do you love Little Miss?" One by one, they began to nod their head yes. Avery went to each of them and rubbed their head and neck. They nuzzled her as if to hug her. Avery could not stop the tears. It was an incredible feeling. "Whoa, this is a great surprise. Thank you so much. I have always loved horses but never owned one." "Well, you own 6 horses right now. And I hope those are happy tears." "Yes, they are. These are my happy tears." Avery said with a giggle. Mr. Peterson walked her back to the house. "Have a great evening." He said with a smile. "Would you like to stay for dinner?" "No, I better get back. Can I have a raincheck?" "Of course you can, sir. And thank you for my surprise. It was so lovely."

Avery went inside and sat down for dinner. Mrs. Ohara had cooked meatloaf, mashed potatoes, and green beans for dinner. It was delicious. While it was not Mrs. Ohara's style of cooking, she cooked what would comfort Avery and make her feel at home. Avery ate until she thought she would burst. The dessert was strawberry shortcake with whipped cream, it was unbelievable.

After she ate, she grabbed a book and headed to her room. She couldn't concentrate because she needed to write down some things from today's experiences. She put the book aside and grabbed her notebook. Only then could she concentrate on the book she wanted to read.

A fleeting thought made her want to see how many emails she had from her publisher but she shushed that thought away. She needed this rest and nothing was going to disturb it. Only she and Samuel knew she had had a slight nervous breakdown in the car that day they met. He had confirmed it when he was here. It would be a long road back to normal and she refused to ever do another book tour for as long as she lived. Samuel called every evening to check on her. Avery had kept the conversations short and noninformative.

She was still not over Samuel expressing negatively about the staff calling her Little Miss. That was just none of his business, and he certainly did not have a say in her life. Avery counted and she had filled up 6 notebooks with story ideas and experiences she has had on the property. 'This place was so special. I feel no stress, no panic, and no anxiety.' She said to herself. It was amazing the way she had gotten the staff to open up to her, without her sharing much information about herself. Avery complimented them every single day and was genuinely happy to see each of them. No one demanded anything from her and they were so kind to her. She had given the assistant time off with pay since she was not wanting to do any dictating or sharing of her work just yet. Avery also felt that the assistant would report to Roger any progress she made. She had that experience before when she took a rest.

Avery couldn't figure out why Roger was pestering her about a work in progress that she hadn't even told him about. When she found out it was the assistant, Avery fired her. That was when Avery was supposed to be resting in Germany. Avery found herself writing more on her computer. She had disabled the internet so she would not be tempted to read any emails, or headlines God forbid about her life. She was in a very good place right now and she wanted to stay there.

Saturday morning, she walked into the stables, and there stood Midnight, a gorgeous jet-black horse. He had a saddle on. Mr. Peterson spoke up and said, "Little Miss, this is Midnight.

He has been away at another farm, being the stud for several mares since before you came home. He is back now to stay. Would you like to ride him?" Avery hesitated for a moment then said, "I think I would like to walk with him. I don't know if I am ready to ride just yet."

Mr. Peterson smiled and handed her the reins and walked with them around the corral for about 30 minutes. Back in front of the barn, Midnight leaned down and allowed Avery to rub him with her bare hands. Avery spoke gently to him. "I've never had a horse friend before I moved here. You are majestic and I feel such a strong connection with you and all 6 of the other horses." Midnight shook his head yes. Avery walked Midnight over to the corral and shut the gate. She spoke softly to the horse, "It's not you sweetheart. You are amazing and I am in awe of you. However, I have some hidden anxiety that I do not want you to feel." Midnight leaned down and hugged Avery, which made her cry. "I don't want to go back to New York. I want to stay here forever." She whispered. Midnight looked into her eyes and touched her nose with his nose.

Once Avery got back from the stables, she took a shower, then went to her room and opened her laptop. She was trying to think of a way she could stay forever. She opened her email and there were at least fifty emails from Roger, her publisher. They were marked, URGENT. 911

please open, Avery this is important. Against her better judgment, she opened the last email that was sent to her from him.

"Dearest Avery, I don't really know where you are, but please stay there. It is chaos here. Your birth parents have sold your childhood story to anyone and everyone that will buy it. They insist you participated and were not attacked. The media is eating this up. Since your adopted mother is deceased, there is no one to corroborate our rebuttal. The hospital and the police will not release reports until you sign these release forms I am attaching. I have a team of attorneys on the job. I need you to electronically sign this release of medical records and police documents and send it back to me so we can get the hospital and police records. I am so sorry this is happening love, but I am so thankful you are not here to witness the media frenzy. Please take care of yourself. Write me another book dear. Love New York."

Her publisher loved to call himself New York. Avery electronically signed the form and returned it to him immediately without a response. She closed her laptop and went down to the dining room for dinner. Her hands were shaking as she tried to eat. Tonight, was fish and chips. It was delicious but Avery was stressed. She ate ½ of her meal and thanked Mrs. Ohara. "You are the best. I appreciate you so much. Could you put it in the microwave and I will finish it later?" She said to Mrs. Ohara. The cook blushed and said, "You flatter me. My head will be too big to get into Mr. Ohara's car." They laughed together, Avery hugged Mrs. Ohara, then she went to her bedroom. She started to open her laptop but then changed her mind. She did not want to see the headlines. The next day, Avery had the driver take her to a nearby town that had an attorney. Farrell Grady was a local attorney. He was a short, heavy man, with bushy eyebrows, no hair and round glasses. He was overly friendly. "How can I be of assistance, young lady?"

"Sir, I home the home at the end of North Andros. I want to buy the property to the right of me. All of it. I need you to speak to the owner and see if they are willing to sell now. Can I hire you to help me with the process? I want this to be done anonymously and immediately."

Avery produced her real identification. He didn't seem to know her name. His eyes widened as he said, "I had no idea this property was for sale." "I don't know that it is. However, I have the ocean to my right and that land to my left. I need the privacy. The price will not be negotiated, I will pay what they ask."

She saw dollar signs in his eyes. Then he said, "Will you want dual citizenship?"

"Not right away, I want to wait a bit before applying for full citizenship. I never plan on going back to the United States."

"I will contact the owners. I know them personally and feel for the right price, they will sell it to you. Once they agree, we can go ahead with the purchase of the acres, however, you will have to apply for citizenship eventually. Why don't you go ahead and fill out the citizenship papers, while I call them, and I will hold the papers until you are ready for me to file them." Avery agreed and he gave her the citizenship forms. She sat in his office for nearly 2 hours filling them out. During the time Avery was filling out the forms, the owner called back and said they wanted 8 million dollars for the land. Avery did not flinch.

"I think that is a fair price for the land." She said with a smile.

Farrel Grady's eyes lit up again as he said, "Of course, my fee will come after the 8 million. I will only charge you only $35,000 (thirty-five thousand) for handling this sale expeditiously. Avery smiled. She remembered an old joke she heard: 'Why don't sharks eat attorneys? Professional courtesy.'

"That is fine Mr. Grady, just get it done. Get me their bank information and I will have the money transferred to them in a few hours."

Mr. Grady wondered, 'Who is this woman that can spend 8 million dollars like she was buying a snow cone at a carnival?' but then he realized he didn't care who she was as long as the payment transactions went smoothly.

Avery called her publisher... "Hello, New York. It's Avery. I need a favor. I need you to transfer 8 million dollars to the account number I am going to give you. It is going to the property owners that I am purchasing from. Their account number is BX$#SD123957.

Also, $35,000 dollars for the attorney, Farrell Grady. His transaction number is JUFRM159753."

"Property?" he asked.

"Yes sir, I'm buying property. And before you ask...yes, I have an attorney here who has done a title search and they are the rightful owners. I just don't want my name to bring the media here and ruin my healing time. I will be in touch.

I believe I can write 200 books here. I should have a book for you by spring. I also need you to sell my New York apartment and send my personal property to me."

"Avery? Are you certain? Are you okay Avery?" he asked sincerely. "Yes, I am better than I have been in years. I will call you when the transaction is complete. They are hand delivering a land title to the attorney I hired here on North Andros. You have the address here of my home to send my belongings to. Bye for now. Love you, and miss you!" and she hung up. Roger was bewildered. Avery had never made a purchase this large, but it was her money, and she had more than she could ever spend.

He kept her secrets and did not let anyone know where she was. As long as she was safe was all that he was concerned with, and that she writes a new book of course.

In less than 2 hours, the monies were transferred, and the paperwork complete, she was now the new owner of 32 acres of land on North Andros. She went home and walked into her office. She sat down at the antique 1940 Underwood typewriter and began writing her new book. She wrote for 5 hours. Mrs.. Ohara poked her head in and said, "All right young lady, that's enough, it's time for dinner." Avery giggled at Mrs.. Ohara and then said, "Yes ma'am. I am at a stopping point."

Dinner was wonderful. Pork chops, rice and gravy, green beans, and corn on the cob. Not to forget the biscuits and tomato gravy. It was a feast. Mrs.. Ohara stood near the kitchen door so she could hear Avery oooh and ahhh about her food.

She loved feeding people. It was her calling, almost like a ministry. Her mother and grandmother had taught her everything she knew. From the time she was old enough to stand in a chair in front of the stove and the sink, she was following orders on how to cook this and that. She wasn't just an island cook; she had learned the America food by cooking for other Americans that came to visit the Bahamas. She was so glad that she had learned the recipes that Avery loved and mastered them. She was an incredible baker as well. It was no wonder Mr. Ohara adored her so.

Writing on an antique typewriter was more difficult than a laptop or a desk top computer but sometimes Avery just craved the authenticity of the old fashion ways. She didn't have time to constantly stop and deal with corrections. She just wrote, and then she scanned the pages into her desktop. Corrections could be made at any time.

Breakfast was delicious as always. Avery went to sit on the beach afterward, she took a little nap and actually slept for 2 hours. When she woke up, she went back outside. She noticed the sky was different. It looked like rain was coming.

Samuel called her cell phone and told her he was on the way to see her. "I am at the Miami airport right now waiting on my charter plane."

Avery realized she was glad he was coming. She had been hiding her feelings about the news Roger gave her regarding her birth parents and she thought she should to talk to Samuel about it.

The beach waves were a little more aggressive than normal. Avery decided she would ask her staff if a storm was coming. She walked back to the house only to see the lawn manager, Jernigan closing the shutters. "What is going on Jernigan?" "There is a storm heading this way Little

Miss. I am just preparing the house against any wind damage." She helped Jernigan bring in the potted plants on the veranda and put the patio furniture in the shed. He assured her he had it under control but she insisted on helping. Avery instantly thought of Samuel and called him again. His cell phone went to voice mail. He arrived an hour later. He was visibly shaken up by the airplane ride from Miami to North Andros.

"The weather was horrible. The turbulence was violent and made me sick. You better appreciate the fact that I am falling in love with you or I would have demanded that pilot turn that plane around."

Avery ignored the falling in love part of his love announcement but frowned and said, "Oh, my goodness. I am so thankful you are okay. That must have been terrible. I can't believe the pilot would agree to fly in this weather." Samuel smiled sheepishly when he said, "Some people will do anything for money." Avery's mouth was agape, "You mean you paid him extra to make the trip." Samuel nodded yes and sighed. "I'm guilty. I had to see you, especially if you might be in danger of a storm." "Well, this is my first storm on an island. The staff has all but assured me that we will all be safe."

"We will be safe together," Samuel said, as he sat down in the nearest chair. He looked green as a leaf of a palm tree, and Avery felt bad for him. "Avery dearest, would you mind getting me a drink of anything that has alcohol? My nerves are a little stretched right now." "Of course, Samuel." Avery found the bar and poured a shot of peach schnapps. She brought it to him and he downed it.

He smiled at her and said, "Thank you so much dear, that was entirely disgusting, but hopefully, it will help me to calm down. I thought several times we were going to crash and die. I was scared I would never see your pretty face again." Avery sat next to him and held his hand. "You are safe now. Promise me you won't try any more daredevil tricks?"

He shrugged his shoulders and said, "I can't make a promise I am bound to break. A man in love knows no boundaries." Avery smiled, ignored his statement and said, "I am just so glad that you are okay."

Mrs.Ohara called them to the dinner table. She had chicken broth, hot tea, and buttered crackers for Samuel. "This will nurse you back to health sir." Mrs. Ohara said as she put a blanket around him. He was still visibly shaking. Avery ate chicken strips and a Greek salad. After dinner, Mrs. Ohara asked if she could leave a little early. "I'd like to be with my husband during the storm if that is acceptable to you. He is a veteran and his nerves are not steady during lightning parts of storms." Avery said, "But of course Mrs. Ohara. Go and be with your husband. I will take care of everything here."

Mrs. Ohara said, "Thank you, Little Miss. These summer storms come often in this month but usually don't cause much damage. Hurricanes are scary but we always make it through safely." Mrs. Ohara called her husband to come and take her home. Before she left, she said to Avery, "There is plenty of prepared food, bottled water, and candles should you need them. Keep your cell phone charged. I should be back in less than 2 days."

Samuel told her, "Take all the time you need dear Mrs. Ohara. If I can help with your husband, please let me know. Remember I am a medical doctor."

She smiled curtly and said, "Yes sir, I will remember that information. Be sweet to our Little Miss. We love her very much." Samuel said, "Then it is unanimous, we all love her." Avery hugged Mrs. Ohara goodbye. "Please be safe Mrs.. Ohara." She and Samuel went outside to the deck to look at the clouds. They were gorgeous, dark grey and white against the blue water. Suddenly Avery remembered Mr. Peterson and the horses.

"Samuel, I need to ride over to the horses and see Mr. Peterson to see if he wants to join us at the house. I will be right back." "Do you want me to go with you dear?" He was thankful when she answered, "No, you stay and rest. It won't take long."

Mr. Peterson was surprised to see Avery. "Young lady, what are you doing out in this potential weather?"

"I just came to bring you some dinner, and ask if you wanted to take shelter in the house during the storm."

"Thank you very much for the offer. I always stay with the horses no matter the weather. I have a room here at the stables that is safe. Again, thank you so much for the offer. I don't think this storm will be as bad as they say. I have been watching the radar, and I feel like it will turn and miss us completely, leaving us with heavy showers and some wind. I truly don't see any damage in our immediate future, however, please stay inside the house and out of the elements. Lightening can strike at any time."

She grabbed Mr. Peterson's arm and said, "I am truly grateful for you. I have never known anyone so kind and responsible for animals."

He smiled and said, "Back to the house with you, Little Miss. Thank you for the dinner. If you need me, I am here."

Avery hurried back to the house. As she entered her house she heard Samuel, moaning. He was stretched out on the couch

"Are you okay Samuel?" she called out to him.

"No, the room is spinning. I think the plane ride over has zapped my strength. I think a good night's sleep will revive me. Will you forgive me if I retire early?" "Of course, Samuel, I just want you to feel better. Now remember we have a storm headed this way so I may wake you up to protect me." Avery said with a giggle. Not finding the humor she was trying to give...

He responded, "That will be fine my dear." He stumbled to the guest bedroom. Avery checked on him ten minutes after he went to the room. He was out like a light, snoring softly.

Avery settled in to do more writing. The words were flowing like a fountain. She had changed from the antique typewriter to her desktop computer. She had probably been writing for 2 hours when she heard the first rumble of thunder. She immediately turned off the computer and went to unplug everything that was plugged in. Those were the instructions Mrs. Ohara had left.

While unplugging the television in the living room, Avery heard a strange buzzing noise. She walked around trying to find where the sound was coming from. It was in the sofa, under one of the cushions. She prayed it wasn't a bug making that noise. Avery reached down and dug it out. It was a cellphone. She opened it to try and turn it off. There was a text message to Samuel.

"Doctor Samuel (Hahaha you a doctor) Don't forget we are paying you for information on Miss High and Mighty. You should have enough by the end of this trip for us to forge ahead with the defamation lawsuit, and then you can go back to your miserable life as a shoe salesman and back to your ugly wife and kids. Hurry up!"

Avery was shocked. The man who had listened to her about her past was an imposter and was working for someone, probably her biological parents to trap her so they could sue her for defamation of character. He would be their star witness. Not to mention, he was masquerading as a doctor and had started telling her that he was falling in love with her. She suddenly remembered her driver who had recommended him, who said he was his cousin. He was in on this scheme too. Avery immediately telephoned New York, her publisher, and told him to fire the driver with a quickness and give no letter of reference. Then she explained about Samuel and the text message on the cellphone. Avery said, "I can't make him leave yet; we are preparing for a storm here. I am not scared Roger, I am disappointed. He seemed like such a nice man, but he was a real good actor. I believed him completely. As soon as the weather clears, I will have the island authority's escort him from here and tell him not to return. I guess I am destined to be alone for the rest of my life."

"Sweetie please don't say that. Somewhere there is a man who is real and will love you for you. I would do it but you know my husband doesn't allow me to date."

Avery chuckled and said, "I suppose it's the thought that counts Roger. I will let you know when Samuel is gone from here." "Okay, kitten. Please be safe. Keep your phone with you in case you need to call for help."

"I will Roger. Talk to you soon, the rain is coming in hard." Avery hung up the telephone and sat down in a nearby chair. She couldn't help but feel so many emotions, but betrayal and humiliation were the main ones. She took 2 books out of her library that she had been wanting to reread. Both were written by one of her favorite authors Francine Rivers. She loved anything by Francine. They had met several times and instantly liked each other. They had tea in London, and chatted like old friends. It was a great memory for her. New York had orchestrated the entire meeting. A perfect gift for her birthday. One she will never forget. She has a picture of the two of them together in the tea room. They were both holding each other's books that they had exchanged as gifts. It was one of her favorites.

She also met J.K. Rowlings and was fascinated by her. She was kind, yet outspoken. That was a wonderful day as well.

Avery wondered if the other authors had suffered any disappointments in their lives, as bad as she had.

Avery took the books to her room and locked the door behind her. She put her cell phone on the charger so it would have a full charge in case she needed to call for help. The storm raged on for hours. She could hear the wind raging outside, but she did not have the courage to look out at the ocean. Avery thought she might panic if she saw that. She said a prayer for Mr. Peterson and the horses. Then she immersed herself into the book she was reading. Avery finally fell asleep at about 430 in the morning as the wind quit howling. At 8 o'clock in the morning, she woke up and went to check for damage. The storm had passed. The house did appear not to have any damage. There were palm tree branches in a pile, but nothing major. She walked down to the stables to see Mr. Peterson. He was brushing a horse. He smiled when he saw her.

"Good morning, Little Miss, so what did you think of your first storm?" "It wasn't as bad as I imagined it would be. The house doesn't have any damage. Thank goodness."

"Yes, I know, I went there to check when the sun came up."

"You made the pile of branches?" she asked.

"Guilty. I will haul them off, when they dry, and I will burn them." "Thank you so much."

"It's all part of the job. I wouldn't expect you to get out there and drag those limbs. They are quite heavy and will cut you if you don't use gloves. It will be a couple of weeks before the landscape people come back. I don't mind helping out." Avery thanked him again. "May I help brush the horses?"

"Yes ma'am. Do you remember where the brushes are?" "I do." Avery needed something to take her mind off of Samuel and his deception. So, Mr. Peterson, when will the plane be able to go back to Miami?" He chuckled and asked, "You had enough of us already?" Avery sighed and said, "Mercy no. I have a visitor in my guest bedroom that I want out of my house as soon as possible."

Mr. Peterson's face changed to a concerned and he asked, "Do you want me to come over there and put him out? He hasn't hurt you, has he?"

"Not physically no, but he pretended to be a doctor so I took him into my confidence, like an idiot. He has been pretending to be my friend, even saying he was falling in love with me. His cell phone fell in between the cushions of the sofa when he was lying on it. He went to bed early. I didn't know what was making a buzzing noise. It was driving me crazy. When I finally found it, it was a cellphone, his, and there was a text message, exposing him. I slept with my door locked last night, the few hours I slept. I don't think he is dangerous. I think he is greedy and looking for a payout."

Mr. Peterson's face was bright red, as he was incensed with anger. "Now Little Miss, I would never get into your business unless you wanted me to, but I think we should call the Royal Police constable to meet us back to your house and evict this pathetic man. If he thinks you are onto him; he might get desperate and hurt you." Avery shook her head yes and wiped the tears from her eyes. "I know you are right. I am not an actress so I couldn't pretend I don't suspect anything. The only thing I could do is write about him in a story, and then kill him off." Mr. Peterson laughed out loud, "Ha! That is one solution. But characters like him have a way of showing up repeatedly. That is why I didn't suggest you pay him or anyone else off. He would keep coming back for more money after a certain amount of time."

Mr. Peterson called his friend at the Royal Bahamas Police Force, Captain Bree. He explained the situation to him. Captain Bree said he would meet them at Avery's house in 15 minutes.

When Mr. Peterson and Avery arrived at the house, Captain Bree was in the living room speaking with a disoriented Samuel. Samuel was in handcuffs. He looked like he just woke up. Avery could hear him telling the captain, "I'm telling you that you have the wrong man. Ask the owner of this house." Avery coughed to make her presence known. Samuel turned around and said, "Thank God Avery. Tell them I am Doctor Samuel Marteen from New York." Avery stared at him for a second, then said, "According to the text that I accidentally read on your cell phone, you are here to gather information about me and you are selling that information to someone.

They said you are not a doctor but a shoe salesman, and you are married with children." Samuel sat back on the sofa. The captain showed Avery several papers that were warrants for Samuel's arrest from the America. The picture was him, however, there were 6 different alias names, one was Samuel Marteen.

"This man has fraud warrants in 5 different states in the United States. The FBI will travel here to transport him back there for prosecution." The captain's constable made him stand up. Samuel turned to Avery and said, "I'm sorry. I truly was falling in love with you."

Through gritted teeth, Mr. Peterson said, "Get him out of here before I break his face." The constable walked him out of the house and took him to their jail cell to await extradition. As Avery watched them drive away, she said, "You know Mr. Peterson, as many books as I have written, I could never have made this stuff up." He stood next to her and said, "Little Miss, this world is full of givers and takers. Thank goodness you found out sooner than later about that idiot. This situation could have been a lot worse dear. The takers take all you let them take." Avery wiped a tear away and said, "Yes sir you are right. Ive been a giver all of my life."

"Do you want to go back to the stables with me?" "No, I am going to stay here and maybe write a little bit. I haven't had much sleep so I will probably catch a nap also." "Okay, if you need me don't hesitate to call." "Thank you so much. You rescued me today. I will always remember what you did for me."

Mr. Peterson gave her a small smile and tipped his hat to her, as he walked back to the stables. Avery settled down for a well-deserved nap. She reached for the bottle of pills that Samuel had prescribed her, then she recoiled from the bottle. She had no idea what the pills were since he was not a doctor. She finally convinced herself to take them to the local clinic after her nap. Mr. Peterson drove her to the clinic. The doctor on duty studied the pills and found out they were nothing more than coated regular aspirin. "Aspirin? Then why did it relax me?" Avery asked.

The doctor said, "I am not trying to be unkind dear, but when we are stressed out, we can convince ourselves that a magic pill will fix us. That man just played on your situation. Aspirin is good to ward off a heart attack and can aid with chest pains at times. We should just thank God, he didn't give you poison, right?"

Avery blushed and said, "Yes sir. You are correct, but in my defense, he did tell me he was a doctor."

The doctor pointed to his wall, where his medical degree was hanging. "Next time you will investigate more, right?"

Avery laughed and said, "Yes sir, I will."

When they left Mr. Peterson drove Avery around the island. There were limbs down but no major damage.

Avery said, "Well at least people didn't lose power." Mr. Peterson said, "Little Miss, many people lost power during the storm. You didn't because you have huge generators that keep the power on at your house." Avery's mouth fell open as she said, "I had no idea."

"It's not a big deal. The government offered smaller generators to the population here years ago. A few families accepted the offer, others were insulted and refused them."

"Why would they be insulted?"

"Because a lot of people do not trust the government and would rather suffer than accept anything from them."

Avery's eyes were wide. Mr. Peterson had to laugh. "It's okay Little Miss. To each his own."

Avery said, "I want you to find out who does not have a generator and I am going to donate one to those people who don't have one. The note will say, "Not from the government but from a lady who loves this island and its people."

Mr. Peterson smiled and said, "Yes ma'am. I will get right on that. I have a friend who works in the utility department. He will help me find out the addresses of those who need one. I love your generous spirit. I think that is why the horses love you. They really can tell who has a good heart and who is not worth their time."

Avery touched Mr. Peterson's arm and said, "Thank you for all you do. I have a feeling we are going to be friends forever."

"We have to be, I don't want you to write about me and kill me off in your story." Avery laughed, "I'll be watching you, sir."

When they arrived back at Avery's house, Mrs. Ohara was shaking out some rugs. "You didn't have to rush back Mrs. Ohara." "Oh, it was no rush. Not much lightning, so Mr. Ohara was calm. I have your dinner ready." Avery asked, "Mr. Peterson will you please stay and eat dinner with me? It's been a heck of a day and I'd rather not be alone." "I will but then you have to come with me to feed the horses." "It is a deal!"

Mrs. Ohara had stew with carrots, potatoes, and fresh bread prepared. It was delicious. She also made a beautiful fruit salad for dessert.

Avery and Mr. Peterson drank coffee and looked over the water. "Where did the storm actually hit?" Avery asked.

"Miami and up the East Coast got the worst of it. It wasn't a hurricane, just a storm. For every 25 amazing and beautiful days here, we have a storm. It averages out. Usually, we get the winds and rain from the outside of the storm, but there are times when hurricanes come right through us."

Avery looked off in the distance and said, "I would rather face these storms than the media storm that is going on in the States about me. Why do people thrive on gossip and lies about people they barely know?"

"Because they don't have interesting lives Little Miss. So, they live for gossip."

"I am so happy here. I feel safe and at home. It's like nothing can touch me." "I promise you Little Miss, you have never been safer." He smiled as he said it, "Now we have some beautiful animals waiting on us for some food and attention" Avery smiled and said, "Away we go!" They rode back to the stables on Mr. Peterson's ATV. Avery was surprised how natural it felt to hold on to his waist as they rode. She did feel safe with him. The horses were nodding when they saw Avery. She said, "Hello everyone! Are we ready to eat?"

The horses all nudged their feed buckets and made neighing sounds. Avery filled their buckets with food and Mr. Peterson filled the water buckets. Once they finished eating, each one was brought out for brushing and cuddling. Avery realized that she was truly at peace. She looked over her shoulder at Mr. Peterson and they smiled at each other.

Two hours later, when every horse was fed, watered, brushed, and walked, Avery said, "Good night, sir. I'm going home to write." "Please let me give you a ride back to the house." "Okay, if it is not an interrupting you. I'm kind of sore from walking on the beach so much. I am really out of shape." "It is no problem at all Little Miss. I quite enjoy your company. And listen, you can call me Stephen. Mr. Peterson was my father." Avery repeated his name, "Stephen. That name suits you." He laughed and said, "Good thing, I have had it all my life."

On the ride back to the house, she told him about buying the property next to her house. "I just wanted the privacy. I have the ocean to my left and now acreage to my right. Maybe tomorrow you will feel like riding over there so I find my property line."

Stephen said, "I would love to ride you over there. Just call me when you are

ready." He reached into his wallet and pulled out a card with his cell number on it. "In case you misplaced the other piece of paper I wrote my number on." Avery said, "Thank you Mr. Pete..um Stephen."

She went home, sat at her computer, and spent the next 5 hours writing. The words were flowing very well and time got away from her. Writing had always been that way for her, feast or famine. Either she could write 8000 words, or could not write 5 that made sense. It was about midnight before she went to sleep, but she slept well for the first time in a while.

Mrs. Ohara had a beautiful breakfast cooked for her. It was soul-touching. Not many cooks could touch Avery's soul, the center of her universe, but Mrs. Ohara could with almost every meal she prepared. Avery checked her email after breakfast. There was one from Mr. Grady, the attorney who handled the property purchase. He had a long-drawn-out letter of appreciation and reminded her if she ever needed him, that he considered himself her personal attorney. Avery just shook her head and said, "I hope I don't need his services again. I could tell he was a shyster. I should include him in one of my stories." Then she laughed and said to herself, 'No is the kind of man who would sue me just to make a name for himself. However, I could write a children's story about a weasel who stole from neighbor's gardens and model it after him.' Avery laughed again.

She called Stephen and he arrived to escort her around her new property.

"Will you please have one cup of coffee with me?"

Stephen smiled and said, "Of course I will. Mrs. Ohara makes wonderful coffee."

Avery noticed Stephen had brought his truck to take her to see her new purchase. "Where is the ATV?" she asked curiously.

"I didn't bring it because the land you purchased may have snakes or other reptiles that we need protection from, protection an ATV would not provide." "Snakes?" Avery yelped. "I better not have purchased snakes on that property. That is not acceptable."

Stephen laughed and said, "Little Miss Mother Nature does not seek or require our permission or approval. Hopefully, there are owls and other exotic birds and fingers crossed, no reptiles. However, I cannot promise there are no reptiles." "I certainly hope not. I am very terrified of rats and snakes." "Oh no! We do have what is called, Bahamian Hutia, it is a rabbit-sized rat-like mammal but it is in danger of becoming extent. It is against the law to kill it, but cats, dogs, and mongoose will kill one if they see it. They don't abide the law."

Avery shuttered. A rabbit sized rat? She shuttered again. "We also have 12 different kinds of snakes and deadly spiders, but they don't come into the populated areas very much, as they are not fond of horses who will stomp on them immediately when they see them. Are you planning on building on that property?"

"No, I just want it for the privacy. Maybe a fence one day to keep strangers out." "Well, if you don't disrupt the footprint of the land, it won't force the occupants to move elsewhere." Avery looked a little green. Stephen said, "Little Miss, I give you my word, I will protect you." Avery smiled and said, "Okay, I will remember that. Don't be mad when I call you to kill a spider." Stephen pretended to bow to her and said, "It would be my honor."

They headed out on their adventure. The sky was beautiful, the water was crystal clear. Stephens's truck drove easily through the sand. He knew the area, like the back of his hand so he was able to show her the property lines that were now hers. It was a fun-filled few hours. There were all kinds of exotic birds, that Avery loved. She wished she had brought her camera.

"Stephen, could we come back another day, so I bring my camera? I would love to take pictures of all of the birds. They are so beautiful."

He smiled and answered, "Just say when and we will come back. I didn't know you were a photographer."

"I'm just a novice. I always wanted to create a coffee table book of photographs but I always chicken out. I don't even know if people use coffee tables anymore." Stephen laughed and said, "Surely coffee tables are not obsolete. I have always had one. As a matter of fact, I built one to go in my living space above the stables."

"You built it?" "Yes, you will find I am quite handy. One day I will show it to you." "I would like to see it," Avery said with a smile.

When they arrived back at Avery's home, 2 ladies were waiting to see her. One older and one younger. Stephen immediately spoke up, "Hello, can we help you?"

The older lady spoke up, "Mrs. Ohara has taken ill all of a sudden. She called and asked that Nicole and I, I'm Mrs. Jefferson. Nicole is my niece, she asked that we come and assist Ms. Lawson." "Certainly, we are glad to have you. I pray Mrs. Ohara is okay. Please have a seat and wait right here. We will get us some refreshments." Stephen said as he escorted Avery inside.

"Call Mrs. Ohara right now to make sure they are legitimate." Avery dialed her number and Mr. Ohara answered. "Hello, Ohara residence. "Hello, Ohara residence. Who is calling?" "Hello, Mr. Ohara. This is

Avery Lawson. Is Mrs. Ohara there?" "Of course not! She is at your house working. You haven't seen me pick her up yet, have you?"

"No sir. I was out away from the house. If you would please drive over here now." Mr. Ohara hung up the telephone. Stephen telephoned the constable immediately and asked them to come quickly. Avery came back out and asked the ladies to enjoy the view of the ocean as she put a pitcher of lemonade and 4 glasses down.

"I need to know a little about you and explain what kind of work you will do here." She shook her head no to Stephen to let him know something was wrong. He went into the house and looked around for Mrs. Ohara. Her purse was in the pantry but she was nowhere to be found.

"So, Mrs. Jefferson do you live on the island?" "Yes, dear. Nicole lives with me. She is my eldest child." Nicole looked down but did not say anything. Mrs.Jefferson had previously said Nicole was her niece.

"Did Mrs. Ohara explain any of your tasks as cook and housekeeper?"

"No, she just said, you were very nice and easy to get along with." Avery smiled and said, "That was very kind of her to say. I love Mrs. Ohara. She is like a mother to me. Do you have experience with American food, and housekeeping?"

"Yes, I have years and years of domestic experience. I have trained Nicole to assist me. She is an excellent cleaner and I do all the cooking." "That is so wonderful. The work here is not demanding. Some light cleaning and some cooking are all that is involved. Mrs. Ohara bless her heart makes it all look so easy. I just adore her. She is like a mother to me, always making sure I am okay. Mrs. Jefferson smirked, "So if anything happened to her you would pay just about anything huh?"

"No not just about anything, I would pay ANYTHING to get her back safely." Nicole lifted her blouse and showed a small gun in her waist band. Avery said, "I understand. Is there a ransom?"

Mrs.Jefferson said, "Don't be vulgar. It is called a donation. WE will call you later tonight, to tell you where to leave the donation." Avery was trying to keep them there as long as she could. "Wait, I have to know that she is okay. She has a husband. Can I speak to her?"

Mrs. Jefferson sharply said, "No, I have this though." It was a tape recorder. She pressed play and it was Mrs. Ohara's voice. "Little Miss, I am okay, except for a bump on my head. It is not too bad. Tell Mr. Ohara I love him in case something bad happens to me. I..." then the recording stopped.

Stephen thought he heard Mrs. Ohara's voice but did not see her when he came out to the patio.

Avery spoke up, "Stephen darling, will you get my medication? I am on the brink of a migraine. It is in the kitchen." "Yes love, of course." He said sweetly.

As soon as he arrived in the kitchen the constable was at the back door. "I have no idea what is going on. I think Mrs. Ohara may have been kidnapped. Avery is on the porch with 2 strange women. They initially said Mrs. Ohara was sick and sent them in her place to work."

The constable and his partner followed Stephen outside to the patio. Avery calmly said, "The younger one has a gun. She showed me." The constables tackled her and got the gun away from her. It was a toy gun. Then they grabbed Mrs. Jefferson and checked her for a weapon. They took the tape recorder from her and handcuffed them both.

Avery started screaming. "They have kidnapped Mrs. Ohara They have a recording of her." Both women were taken into custody. The investigator who had just arrived said to the handcuffed women, "It would be in your best interest to tell us where Mrs. Ohara is at, or you will suffer the dire consequences." The older woman said, "I don't have her. I was hired by a man to come here and let Ms. Lawson know that she has been kidnapped." "Who is the man?" "I don't know." "What does he look like?"

"I don't know, he contacted me by telephone."

"She's lying." the younger woman said calmly, not looking up.

The investigator walked up to the older woman and directly in her face, said, "I will make sure you serve every minute of your sentence if you do not give us facts instead of fantasy."

She sighed, then said, "He is older, white hair, kinda heavy. He cusses a lot and smells like liquor. He told me that Ms. Lawson owes him a lot of money and he intends to get it all back from her."

"How much did he pay you?"

"Nothing yet. He promised one million pounds to us."

Avery collapsed into Stephen's arms. He took her to the bedroom and sat her on the

bed. One of the constables came in and asked her did she know who the kidnapper

was and she said, "I am 100% sure it is my biological father. He has been after my

money and this is his way of tormenting me. I am sure Samuel told him where I

live and about Mrs. Ohara."

Mr. Ohara was calling out from the kitchen. Stephen and the constable went to explain the situation to him. They had to call emergency services for him. He collapsed.

The women were in the back of the patrol vehicle. The constable pulled out the youngest one. "Is this your real mother?"

"No, she stole me when I was a baby. I guess she raised me. She is very mean to me and uses me in her criminal activities." "Do you know where Mrs. Ohara is being kept Nicole? We need to find her before she dies."

"We came over on a private boat from the next island over. I think the man took the older lady you call Mrs. Ohara to that island and hid her."

"Thank you for your cooperation, Nicole." "My name is Agnes. She just calls me Nicole."

Stephen and one of the constables tried to comfort Mr. Ohara. He refused to go to the hospital. He wanted to wait to get his wife back. Avery insisted he lie down in her guest room until they found Mrs. Ohara. The Royal Police arrived in their boat. They took the 2 women to the next island to look for the kidnapped Mrs. Ohara. The United States had faxed a recent picture of Avery's biological father. He was the number one suspect. The younger woman identified him as the master mind behind the kidnapping. The constable asked, "How is he supposed to get in touch with you when you receive the ransom money?"

"I am to meet him on the main Pier and hand over the bag of money." The older woman said with a sigh. The 2 women looked at each other, sharing a look. They were not telling them everything. The constable said, "I think it is important to tell you that if you withhold any information, I will charge you with perjury and interfering with an investigation. Also, if the victim is harmed or God forbid killed, you will share the exact sentence with the man, that you say is behind this."

The younger woman spoke up, "She is supposed to wear a red shirt when she walks on the pier. Any other color would alert the man that law enforcement is around and he will not come and get the money. He will be wearing a blue shirt. He has white hair and is fat. However, he said he may be wearing a brown wig as a disguise."

The older woman groaned and said, "Thanks a million you ungrateful, snitch." "I'm not going to prison for you Leanna. You have tormented me my entire life. This situation is the straw that breaks the camel's back."

The constable radioed ahead and had someone bring a red shirt for the older woman. She grumbled, "I don't know why I am helping you." The constable nearly hissed at her, "Because you will be sorry if you don't help us. We don't tolerate kidnappers or murders on these islands. You will not sully our good names and reputations."

Back at Avery's, Mr. Ohara was drinking a cup of coffee. His hands were shaking badly, he was spilling most of it. He had cried until he was feeling sick. Stephen asked if he wanted to lie down again and he nodded yes. He put the coffee cup down and begged Stephen, "Please find my wife. Please." Stephen assured him that the Royal Police were handling the investigation. Then he helped him to the bed. Mr. O'Hara stretched out and started praying aloud. Avery had been crying too. Stephen called in 2 of his friends from another island to attend to the horses while he stayed at the house with Avery. "Please don't make yourself sick honey. They will find Mrs. Ohara and she will be mad but happy to be back. After they catch the man behind this, I am going to hire security for you. I don't know why I didn't think of this sooner. That bit with the famous doctor/ salesman, Samuel, should have made me realize more was to come."

"Stephen please don't blame yourself. This is the doing of a madman. We didn't know how far he would go, but now we do. I agree with you. I think security will help a lot to give us a piece of mind. I'm sorry that you have to be away from the horses tonight. Wont they be lost without you being there with them?" "It will be fine dear. I called in Hector and Ignacio. They are friends of mine who have helped with the horses before. They know how to care for them."

"Thank goodness. I know they need good care. You always do a fantastic job."

The woman known as Mrs. Jefferson (Leanna) was told to act as the kidnapper would expect her. "Do not deviate from the plan. Do not light a cigarette. Do not try to signal him in any way or I swear we will prosecute you for the entire kidnapping. We want that elderly lady back in one piece." Leanna said, "I understand. I am not going down for this alone." She stood on the pier with her red shirt on, holding a large duffle bag. It was filled with rocks, to imitate it was filled with a lot of money. One of the agents was fishing off of the pier, acting like he was lost in his fishing, and pretending to ignore the woman. His hat had a tiny camera in the back so he could record whoever arrived to get the ransom money. There were also 4 agents pretending to clean a Schiffer that was parked in a slip next to the pier. The man appeared in his blue shirt and brown wig. The agents surprised him, pouncing on him and taking him down quickly. They separated him and the elderly woman and took their statements. They took the man immediately to the nearest Royal Police Station and put him in an interview room. The man denied any knowledge of the kidnapping. One of the constables grabbed him by his shirt and threw him into the wall. "Give us your bloody full name." The man gave a false name. "Bill Smith." The constable was furious. He screamed, "We have your correct name from the United States, try again." "John Flagman."

"You will tell us where Mrs. Ohara is now, and she better not be hurt or dead, because here in the Bahamas, you are fed from the same spoon you feed others with."

Blood was coming from the man's eye, from being thrown into the wall. He assumed he might get a proper beating from these police and he also knew he was too old to take that beating.

"Where is Mrs.Ohara?" John Flagman hesitated but saw the constable ball up his fist and walk towards him. "Okay, okay. Wait, she uh ... She is in a storage shed here on this island. Number 1507. I will take you there."

"Not necessary." The Investigator said as he radioed for the local agents to go to the storage shed, and take bolt cutters for the lock.

"Okay, Mr. John Flagman. Tell us your story. Again, honesty, is the best policy with our agency. We don't tolerate liars, thieves or men that kidnap innocent women." John swallowed hard and said, "My daughter lives on North Andros Island. She is stinking, filthy rich and refuses to give me any of her money. I have begged and pleaded for financial assistance from her. She and her publisher refuse me any communication or money. This was the act of a desperate man. I am dying and I need her help."

Mr. Fieldman was not dying; it was just part of his story. He was trying to gain sympathy from the officers. The investigators asked for his doctor's name in America. Mr. Flagman looked surprised that they would ask that, then said, "Doctor Samuel Marteen." The officers laughed in his face and said, "Mr. Flagman, we know that you partnered up with Samuel to try and extort money from Ms. Lawson.

The FBI is on its way to extradite you for that charge. The kidnapping charge will then be tried in London in Queen Elizabeth's court. So, you are probably looking at a total of 50 years between the multiple charges."

John Flagman was speechless. He looked pale. The investigator's radio beeped and he was told they had Mrs. Ohara and she was being transported to the hospital. "She has a bad head wound, and is severely dehydrated and mad as hell." An accompanied constable used the telephone to call Avery and let her know they had Mrs. Ohara and she was alive.

"Oh, thank God! Thank God!" Avery said. Stephen went into the guest room to tell Mr. Ohara. He leaped from the bed and shouted, "Glory to God!" then he ran into the living room and begged Avery, "Take me to her." Stephen said, "Yes sir, we will all go to the hospital."

The captain charged John Fieldman with Felony kidnapping, Felony Assault on an elderly person, and Extortion of an elderly person. Each crime was punishable up to 20 years a piece in Queen Elizabeth's courthouse. The constables left to go to the hospital to see if Mrs.. Ohara could give her statement. John Flagman was left in a cell at the police station. Leanna was charged with Felony Conspiracy and Extortion. Her crimes were punishable by 10 years each in Queen Elizabeth's courthouse.

Nicole was charged with aiding and abetting; her crimes were punishable by 5 years' probation, if she cooperated with testifying against John Flagman and Leanna. If she did not cooperate, the 5 years' probation would be converted to 5 years in prison. Nicole agreed to cooperate 100%.

Mrs. Ohara looked exhausted but she was alive. Her husband wept as he ran to her bedside. "My darling. I don't know what I would have done if I lost you." He cried out.

Mrs. Ohara was weak. She calmly said, "Now you stop that Mr. Ohara. I am as good as new. The doctor was here before you arrived. He said I can go home in a few days. He wants to make sure I have plenty of fluids. I sweated a lot in that storage shed."

She turned to Avery and said, "Little Miss, are you okay? The constable said the women approached you for the ransom money?"

Avery smiled and said, "Yes dear, I am fine. We have all been terribly worried about you. We love you, Mrs. Ohara." "I love all of you too." She said with a yawn. "I need to sleep some now. I am rather tired from all of this nonsense."

Mr. Ohara stayed with her. He told the nurse, "I refuse to leave her side again." The doctor made an exception and allowed him to stay.

Avery and Stephen brought some food for the Ohara's because hospitals are famous for having terrible food. Avery also brought flowers to decorate Mrs. Ohara's room. The nurses brought in an extra chair and a cot for Mr. Ohara to sleep in. Stephen and Avery went back to her house. There was a constable there to receive their full statements. The constable looked uncomfortable and said, "I have some interesting news. I am not sure how you will receive this." Stephen told him to tell them the news. The constable said, "John Flagman died of a heart attack while in custody at our police station. He was in a cell waiting for us to come back from seeing Mrs. Ohara. When we returned, he was dead. Our local doctor said it was a massive heart attack." Avery spoke up and said, "Why that is very sad that anyone should die, however, it is of no consequence to me. He gave me away to an orphanage when I was 7 years old."

The constable said, "It's just a shame he didn't live long enough to suffer for his crimes. Hopefully the FBI will take his remains back with them." Avery said, "Well I sure don't want them and I am not responsible for his burial cost either. I was legally adopted by Mrs.Palance at the orphanage." After he left, they were exhausted. Stephen fell slept on the couch and Avery on his shoulder. They slept for about 2 hours. When they woke up, they were holding hands and snuggled up.

There was a knock at the door and Stephen got up to answer it.

It was the head of the security business, Holden and Beats.

"Hello, I'm Cranston Holden. I received your message about wanting to hire security for this property and its owner." "Yes come in please. I'm Stephen Peterson. I will explain the situation."

"Thank you."

Avery went to the restroom to freshen up. She felt like the horrific day had left her looking ragged. She was still exhausted, even after a 2-hour nap.

The 2 men went into Avery's office and Stephen explained the entire situation. "Avery recently bought the acreage to the right side of the house for privacy reasons. However, this is the second breach she has had in her private life due to a lack of security. I feel that she needs a security team. But not one that will scare her or inconvenience her."

"We have a team that she would never see, unless she pushed the panic button we will install. She may get a little traumatized by the amount of security she has on staff. The plan I brought you has mapped out the perimeters, and it shows where the cameras are located. We also provide a bodyguard for when she leaves the property."

Stephen chuckled, "Oh I can protect her, it's the property and access to her through the property that I am concerned with securing."

"Well, just remember that option is available. Just one telephone call and we can

have someone to pose as a driver."

"How long will it take to secure the surroundings?"

"3 days maximum."

"Okay, it sounds like a plan. Where do I sign?"

Mr. Holden handed over the contract. Stephen scanned it, then signed it.

"Mr. Holden, Avery is very important to me. Please remind your men that I am deadly serious about keeping her safe. If anything were to happen to her, I would take it very personally."

"Sir we have 98% success rate. The only reason we don't have a 100% rate was not our fault but the customer's. If you want to hear the details, I will gladly share some of them with you."

"No thank you, Mr. Holden. Just keep my girl safe, when I can't."

Avery walked into her office. She shook hands with Mr. Holden. "Hello, sir. It is nice to meet you."

"You as well. I understand you have had some bad experiences as of late. But believe me when I say my team will secure your property and be available to you should you need us for anything."

"Thank you. I am sure you will take care of us."

The doctors kept Mrs. Ohara in the hospital for 6 days. She had a concussion and a deep cut because she had been hit on the head during the kidnapping. The hospital had rehydrated her by giving her IV bags of saline.

Avery and Stephen had been there every day to check on her. Avery was surprised to see Mr. Ohara wearing hospital scrubs. "When did you start working at the hospital Mr. Ohara?" she teased. He laughed and said, "I ran out of clean clothes and they gave me these to wear after my shower. They are very comfortable. I have 6 pairs of pants and shirts." "Well, you look very professional in them. I can say you do them justice." "I would wear a sheet, just to stay and be near my honey." Mr. Ohara said sweetly. "Oh, you old goat, don't you make me cry. You know I love you." "And I love you, Mrs. Ohara."

It was a touching moment. Stephen reached over and held Avery's hand. She smiled at him and whispered, "Goat". Stephen whispered back, "Nag." Then they giggled. Mrs. Ohara drifted off to sleep, while Mr. Ohara held her hand. Avery asked Mr. Ohara if she could take his clothes and wash them. He smiled and said, "Little Miss, that is sweet of you, but one of the meanest of the nurses already did that. I was completely shocked because she is such a snit, but she showed me favor so I appreciate her now."

The doctor came in and addressed them all. "I am going to release Mrs. Ohara in a few days, but I must be reassured that she will get rest and adequate attention around the clock for at least 4 weeks. It will take that long to make sure she has recovered from the concussion. She has 8 stitches in her head. They will need to be taken out after 6 weeks. She must not do any work, at home or away from home until she is fully recuperated. I know she is hard-headed but you must help her to help herself. I am giving you the telephone number of a local business that is owned by Registered Nurses. They make daily home visits and address any medical concerns. I mean it when I say she needs complete rest. Her blood pressure has been very high. The only reason I am releasing her tomorrow is we have brought the blood pressure down to a reasonable number. I know she has been through a terrible experience."

Avery thanked the doctor. Then she turned to Mr. Ohara. "I am going to call the business and I will pay for everything. I love the two of you."

Mrs.. Ohara was still too weak to argue with the doctor. Avery thanked the doctor. Avery began to cry. "I am just so thankful she is okay. I love you both so much." "We love you too Little Miss." Mr. Ohara said with a smile.

When the company gave the name of the nurse who was coming to assist Mrs.. Ohara, Stephen called Mr. Holden so he could vet the nurse. He only wanted a caring, wonderfully skilled nurse to care for anyone Avery cared about."

After 2 hours, Mr. Holden called back and had cleared the young lady. Stephen also asked him to put a detail of men on Mrs. Ohara's house. The kidnapping had made the news and they didn't want any aggravation brought to Avery or the Ohara's by the media. Thankfully, the news did leave Avery and The Ohara's names out of the segments and articles. The security team was all but invisible to Avery. She felt safer but even more so that Stephen was spending all of his time with her. Every morning and every night they went to the stables to care for the horses, then they would come back to her house and cook together. They went to see The Ohara family every day to check on them. Mrs. Ohara was so ready to come back to work, but the doctor had not released her. Avery paid Mr. Ohara every Friday for Mrs.Ohara's salary and the payment for the nurse. She also sent a lady that would clean and cook for them. Mrs. Ohara did not like that one bit, but she knew that Avery was doing everything out of love.

Mr. Ohara was a little put off by the security being outside, but Stephen explained it was for their protection. The constable did not know if any other criminals were in on the kidnapping plot other than the ones that were arrested. Stephen and Avery just couldn't take the chance of any more kidnapping plots.

Avery hired a separate lady temporarily to cook and clean at her house. Mr. Holden had vetted her and the constables knew the woman personally. Her name was Betsy. She was a great housekeeper and an acceptable cook. They ate a lot more fish with her cooking. Avery missed Mrs. Ohara's cooking terribly.

Sometimes, Stephen would grill steaks and hamburgers sometimes for their dinner. It made Avery feel good watching him grill. She would smile and say, "Don't faint but I am going to try and make a salad and a baked potato for the rest of our dinner." Every time Stephen would laugh and say, "Please poke the potatoes with a fork before you put them in the microwave Little Miss, and don't cut yourself making the salad." She would throw a dish towel at him every time, then pray she did things right. Stephen was seeing that they were a good team. He finally taught her how to ride Midnight. They would ride up and down the beach. It was freeing to Avery to ride this huge horse on the beach. Stephen rode with her. It was amazing to see all of the horses ride freely on the beach.

They were trained to return to the corral when they had their run. In all the time

she had been on North Andros; Avery had never seen the pigs swimming. She

thought she was having a heat stroke and hallucinating.

"Stephen, do you see what I am seeing?"

Stephen laughed and said, "Yes dear, those are the swimming pigs of North

Andros. They are famous, almost as famous as you my dear."

"But in all of this time, I never..."

Stephen laughed and said, "It's okay sweetie. You use your time in various other

ways. This is like a present from your new life."

Avery and Midnight stayed perfectly still as she marveled at the swimming pigs. "Do we own the pigs?" she asked. Stephen said, "The pigs are independent sweetheart. They come and go as they please. Only God owns the pigs." Avery giggled and said, "That was a really foolish question I asked you." Stephen smiled and said, "There are no stupid questions." They rode back to the stable and fed and brushed all of the horses. When they were finished tending to them, they rode the ATV back to Avery's house. "Let's watched a movie on the big screen in the movie room." Avery said, then remembering that she had no idea how to turn it on. It took Stephen a few minutes to figure it out. "Why would you build a house with a theater room in it?" Stephen asked playfully. Avery laughed and said, "You know, my publisher, New York, he designed this house, had it built and even picked out most of the furnishing. All I did was pay for it all when I got the bill." Stephen looked at her and said, "Your publisher's name is New York?" Avery giggled and said, "He is my agent and my publisher. I know its unheard of but he is good at what he does. He calls himself that because he says he owns the city. I never argue with him because I never have the strength to follow through and win." "I really dislike arguing. I am so glad that you and I seem to see eye to eye on everything so far. People don't realize that once they put angry, hurtful words out there, they can never take them back. It damages the foundation of a relationship."

"Stephen! That is the truest statement I have ever heard anyone say. I don't like to argue either. Lord knows I've had my share of bad experiences in my life but now, I just want to be happy for the rest of my life. I can tell in my new writing that it is not as dark as it used to be. I'm learning to tell happier stories." Stephen smiled and said, "As long as you are happy dear." He sat down next to her and pulled her legs into his lap, "Are you happy?" "Deliriously." She purred. "I am truly happy that you are happy Avery. I just want to make sure you are safe and treasured."

Avery giggled, "I think for the first time in my life, I am happy with my life. Of course, New York is going to have migraines when he finds out I am not doing anymore book tours. You know I don't have to write another book if I don't want to, I have made an insane amount of money, and I have made several people and their businesses very rich. However, I write because it is my passion. I feel like I've got so many stories inside of me, begging for me to let them out."

Stephen said, "Little Miss, you are too young to retire, but you are also too intelligent to let the literary world exhaust you. I will support anything you want to do. I just don't want you to leave North Andros." "I have no plans of leaving you. So, mister you are stuck with me!" Avery said with a laugh, "This is the life I have always dreamed of, but never could attain. It was always just out of my reach. New York would tease me and say, 'You can retire one day on your little secluded island, but not today. Today you have a story to tell.' I had only been here 2 times before until this time, now, I have put down roots. I'm home. This may kill New York but I'm home for good." Stephen moved closer to her and took her face in his hands and kissed her. "Avery, I love you. I'm going to spend my time making you happy." "I love you too Stephen." You can write, paint, draw anything you want to, or not, the choices are yours. Like I said, I promise to stand beside you and any decision you make." "And I will stand beside you sweetheart." Avery said, her blue eyes sparkling with love. Stephen kissed her again, then hit play on the remote control. The lights automatically dimmed when the movie started. "You know what Stephen? I have written many, many books, yet I couldn't make up the things we have been through." Avery said with a frown.

"Sweetheart, we are now writing our own love story." Stephen kissed her again, then hit play on the remote control. The lights automatically dimmed and the movie started.

The End

"I love you not because of who you are, but because of who I am when I am with you."

Roy Croft

"Love isn't something you finds you, its something that finds you."
Lorreta Young

Also by Lilly Buchanan

Bad girls
Rahab

King Marc 1
King Marc

Life in a small town
New Life in a Small Town

Standalone
Our Second Chance
Dannie
Leroy
Sugah
The Wright House
Jezebel 2
Kitty's
Murder in Potluch

Writer

About the Author

Lilly Buchanan is originally from Columbus, Georgia. She currently lives in Pascagoula, Mississippi. Lilly started writing when she was a little girl. Lilly loves pretty things, flowers, decorating, writing beautiful stories, volunteering and Jesus! Lilly has 2 amazing granddaughters, Jasmine and Alexandria. If you stop and ask she will show you pictures!!

About the Publisher

Self publishing with Draft to Digital has been an amazing experience.

www.ingramcontent.com/pod-product-compliance
Lightning Source LLC
Chambersburg PA
CBHW051822130726
47987CB00003B/1373